dick bruna

miffy's garden

EGMONT

One day, father bunny

says to Miffy how she's grown,

and now she must be old enough

to have a garden of her own.

Miffy is so happy

and sets out to find some clothes.

Red overalls are perfect,

she will garden well in those.

The earth must be turned over first

and that can take so long,

but luckily her father helps

and he is very strong.

Then it's time to rake the ground

and give it all a shake.

Miffy's very good at this,

she's learned to use a rake.

Then father bunny gives to her

a bag of carrot seed.

He shows her how to sow them

very carefully indeed.

And when the bag is empty,

Miffy rushes off to get

her watering can to sprinkle on

the seeds to make them wet.

Quite soon the plants begin to show

and Miffy can really tell,

that while they are still very small

they're growing up so well.

The little plants are soon quite big,

they've grown so fast with Miffy's care

and when she pulls one up to look

she finds a lovely carrot there.

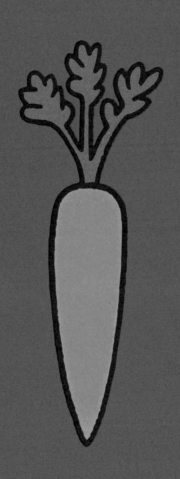

So Miffy gets her basket

and puts all the carrots in,

one by one she piles them up,

some big, some small, some thin.

She takes the carrots to her mum

and what does mother say?

"The carrots look so wonderful,

we'll have a feast today!"

So mother bunny cleans them up

and leaves the carrots whole,

then puts them neatly side by side

together in a bright blue bowl.

And, when there isn't one more carrot

left upon their dinner plate,

they all agree that Miffy's carrots

are the best they ever ate.

miffy's library

miffy's garden
"de tuin van nijntje"
First published in Great Britain 2005 by Egmont UK Limited
239 Kensington High Street, London W8 6SA.
Publication licensed by Mercis Publishing bv, Amsterdam
Original text Dick Bruna © copyright Mercis Publishing bv, 2004
Illustrations Dick Bruna © copyright Mercis bv, 2004
Original English translation © copyright Patricia Crampton, 2004
The moral right of the author has been asserted.
Printed in Germany
All rights reserved
ISBN 978 1 4052 1902 0
10 9 8 7 6 5 4